Dog Gone!

LEEZA HERNANDEZ

G. P. Putnam's Sons • **An Imprint of Penguin Group (USA) Inc.**

ARF = AVID READERS FOR EVER!

G. P. PUTNAM'S SONS • A division of Penguin Young Readers Group. Published by The Penguin Group.
Penguin Group (USA) Inc., 375 Hudson Street, New York, NY 10014, U.S.A.
Penguin Group (Canada), 90 Eglinton Avenue East, Suite 700, Toronto, Ontario M4P 2Y3, Canada
(a division of Pearson Penguin Canada Inc.).
Penguin Books Ltd, 80 Strand, London WC2R 0RL, England.
Penguin Ireland, 25 St. Stephen's Green, Dublin 2, Ireland (a division of Penguin Books Ltd.).
Penguin Group (Australia), 250 Camberwell Road, Camberwell, Victoria 3124, Australia
(a division of Pearson Australia Group Pty Ltd).
Penguin Books India Pvt Ltd, 11 Community Centre, Panchsheel Park, New Delhi - 110 017, India.
Penguin Group (NZ), 67 Apollo Drive, Rosedale, Auckland 0632, New Zealand (a division of Pearson New Zealand Ltd).
Penguin Books (South Africa) (Pty) Ltd, 24 Sturdee Avenue, Rosebank, Johannesburg 2196, South Africa.
Penguin Books Ltd, Registered Offices: 80 Strand, London WC2R 0RL, England.

Design by Marikka Tamura. Text set in Frankie.
The illustrations were rendered in a digital fusion of pencil, acrylic, print, paper and collage.
Library of Congress Cataloging-in-Publication Data
Hernandez, Leeza.   Dog gone! / Leeza Hernandez.   p. cm.
Summary: A dog runs away after getting in trouble, only to be helped home by some friendly strays.
[1. Dogs—Fiction. 2. Lost and found possessions—Fiction.] I. Title.   PZ7.H431777Do 2012   [E]—dc22   2011013408
ISBN 978-0-399-25447-5
10 9 8 7 6 5 4 3 2

For my two top dogs,
Gary and Olivia

Special WOOF!
[of thanks]
to
Tomie,
Cecilia,
Susan
and Pat

Happy dog.

Yappy dog.

Settle down, you snappy dog.

Mad dog.

Sad dog.

Dog gone!

Hurry dog.

Worry dog.

Wandering lost and sorry dog.

Glum dog.

Numb dog.

Pooped-out on-the-run dog.

Enough, dog.

You're tough, dog.

But not for
living rough, dog.

Dear dog.

No more need to fear, dog.

Kissed dog.

schlurp

Best friend can't resist dog.

schlurp

schlurp

No, dog...

Whoa, dog!

I'll never let you go, dog.

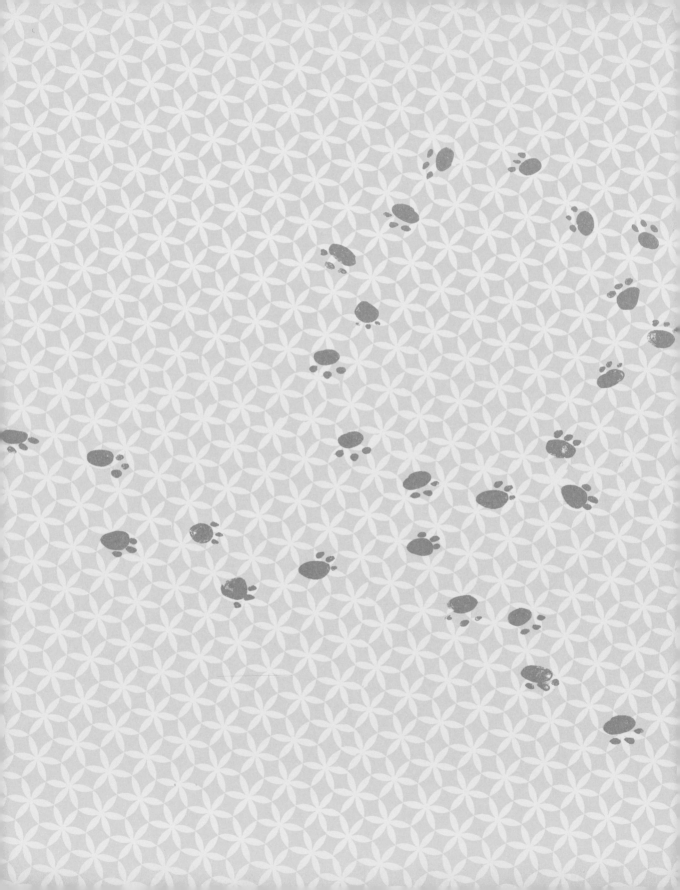